ICK JR
The
ACKYARDIGANS
onics Reading Program

Spot the Frog

by Sonia Sander

SCHOLASTIC INC.

New York   Toronto   London   Auckland   Sydney
Mexico City   New Delhi   Hong Kong   Buenos Aires

"Hi, I am Wizard Tyrone. These are my wizard friends, Uniqua and Pablo. To be Master Wizards, we need to turn a frog into a dog!"

"We have got to find a frog first," said Wizard Tyrone. "I spot a frog in the fog!" called Wizard Pablo.

"This frog won't
stop hopping!"
said Wizard Uniqua.
The frog hopped
into the pond.
Wizard Pablo
hopped in, too.

"I got the frog!"
cried Wizard Pablo.
"Great job!"
said Wizard Tyrone.
"Drop him in this box
so he cannot hop away."

The wizards said:
"*Flip-flop-bop!*"
They turned Wizard Tyrone
into a rock!
"I think we got the
words wrong,"
said Wizard Pablo.
"Let's try again."

The wizards tried:
"*Flip-flop-pop!*"
"Ahhh!" said Wizard Pablo.
"We turned Wizard Uniqua
into a doll!"
"We forgot to nod
our heads," said
Wizard Tyrone.
"Let's try again."

The wizards nodded
and said: "*Flip-flop-pop!*"
The frog popped into a dog.
"We did it!" cried
Wizard Pablo.
"Ribbit! Ribbit!" said the
dog as it hopped away.

"Hooray!" the wizards said.
"We turned the frog into a
dog...a dog that hops!"